BACK FROM NEAR EXTINCTION

GRIZZLY
BEAR

by Tammy Gagne

Content Consultant
Chris Servheen, PhD
Adjunct Research Associate Professor
Dept. of Ecosystem and Conservation Sciences
University of Montana

Core Library

An Imprint of Abdo Publishing
abdopublishing.com

abdopublishing.com

Published by Abdo Publishing, a division of ABDO, PO Box 398166, Minneapolis, Minnesota 55439. Copyright © 2017 by Abdo Consulting Group, Inc. International copyrights reserved in all countries. No part of this book may be reproduced in any form without written permission from the publisher. Core Library™ is a trademark and logo of Abdo Publishing.

Printed in the United States of America, North Mankato, Minnesota
082016
012017

THIS BOOK CONTAINS
RECYCLED MATERIALS

Cover Photo: Shutterstock Images
Interior Photos: Shutterstock Images, 1, 4, 12, 43, 45; Galyna Andrushko/Shutterstock Images, 6; Dieter Hopf/ImageBROKER RF/Glow Images, 9; Wild Living Arts/iStockphoto, 14; Red Line Editorial, 15, 28; Stephen J. Krasemann/NHPA/Photoshot/Newscom, 16; Martin Michael Rudlof/Shutterstock Images, 20; National Park Service, 22; iStockphoto, 25; Darryl Dyck/The Canadian Press/AP Images, 27; Greg and Jan Ritchie/Shutterstock Images, 30; Visual Communications/iStockphoto, 32; Erik Petersen/The Bozeman Chronicle/AP Images, 35; Dougall Photography/iStockphoto, 37; Ken Gillespie/All Canada Photos/Glow Images, 39

Editor: Marie Pearson
Series Designer: Jake Nordby

Publisher's Cataloging-in-Publication Data

Names: Gagne, Tammy, author.
Title: Grizzly bear / by Tammy Gagne.
Description: Minneapolis, MN : Abdo Publishing, 2017. | Series: Back from near
    extinction | Includes bibliographical references and index.
Identifiers: LCCN 2016945430 | ISBN 9781680784688 (lib. bdg.) |
    ISBN 9781680798531 (ebook)
Subjects: LCSH: Grizzly bear --Juvenile literature.
Classification: DDC 599.784--dc23
LC record available at http://lccn.loc.gov/2016945430

CONTENTS

CHAPTER ONE

A GROWING POPULATION

The mother grizzly bear leads her two cubs toward the rushing river. In the months since the new family left the den, the cubs have been eating many new things. Their favorites so far are clover and dandelion greens. Now, the mother is about to give the cubs their first salmon fishing lesson. This spot was where her own mother taught her how to catch fish several years earlier.

Grizzly bears often have twins.

Grizzlies in Alaska sometimes eat salmon.

The cubs stand nearby and watch as their mother waits patiently. The river roars. The mother knows that sometimes salmon will jump right out of the water. But she is too hungry to wait. Instead, she drops one of her massive paws into the water when she sees a fish swimming toward her. She pins it with this simple move. The anxious cubs run over. She walks to the bank with the wriggling fish in her mouth. She will share this catch. But it will be up to the young bears to find their next meal.

The Challenges Grizzlies Face

As many as 100,000 grizzly bears once roamed the western half of North America. This enormous bear species could be found from northern Mexico all the way to the Arctic. More than 50,000 lived in the lower 48 states. By 1975 that number had dropped to less than 1,000. Today the species has completely disappeared from Mexico and the southern United States. They remain in Canada and the northern United States.

What's the Difference?

Some people call the grizzly bear a brown bear. This is neither a mistake nor a nickname. The grizzly bear is actually a North American subspecies of the brown bear. Grizzly bears are found in western Canada, Alaska, Wyoming, Montana, and Idaho. A small number of grizzlies are also thought to live in Washington. The Kodiak bear is the other subspecies of the brown bear in North America. It is found only on the islands of the Kodiak Archipelago in Alaska.

A Big Change

On March 3, 2016, the US Fish and Wildlife Service proposed that the grizzly bears in the Greater Yellowstone Ecosystem be removed from the federal Lists of Endangered and Threatened Wildlife and Plants. The grizzly population there has greatly increased in recent decades. In 1975 only about 136 grizzlies lived in the region. This region includes parts of Montana, Wyoming, and Idaho. Today the area is home to more than 700 of these bears. Many biologists worry that the species will decline again if the government removes federal protections. Without these laws, states could make hunting grizzlies legal again. Some people think hunting could be too much for the grizzly population to sustain.

Conflicts with humans are among the biggest reasons for the grizzly's decline. Over time people have moved onto land occupied by grizzly bears. The construction of homes and businesses has reduced available habitat for bears in much of their range. Grizzly bears adapt quickly to change. They will go wherever they must to find food. Gardens, farms, or even trash can attract these hungry animals. But humans usually dislike the bears' presence. If a bear continues to feed near

Grizzlies may look for food in landfills.

humans, management agencies may relocate or kill the bear.

Climate change has also created some challenges for grizzly bears. One of the bear's primary food sources is whitebark pinecone seeds. These seeds are also called pine nuts. Mountain pine beetles are killing many whitebark pine trees. Warmer temperatures and droughts are making these problems worse.

Whitebark pines are found at high elevations. Cold temperatures used to keep the beetles at lower elevations. But the beetles are moving into the whitebark pine range as temperatures warm. When the air gets warm in spring and fall, the insects are able to reach the taller whitebark pine trees. The beetles kill the adult trees. Still, grizzly bears are resourceful. As pine nuts have disappeared, the bears have found other foods to eat instead. Scientists do not know if these new foods are as nutritious, though.

Despite all these challenges, the grizzly bear species is slowly growing. In 1975 there were as few as 800 grizzlies in the lower 48 states. Today that number has risen to approximately 1,800. The species has been saved from extinction. But there is still work to be done to keep grizzly bear numbers from dropping.

Ecologist Chris Morgan has written about bears on every continent on which they are found since 1991. In a 2011 interview, he discussed what he learned about grizzly bears in Alaska:

> These animals, in many parts of the world, are really highly threatened and in trouble. You look to Alaska and you feel like this is the last place in the United States where at least the near future is secure for these bears. I live in Washington State; we've got about 20 grizzly bears here. I work on that population and I work with members of the public in these rural towns in grizzly bear country to help them understand what grizzly bears are, what we need to do to have more of them here, how we can live with bears. I live that every day, so going to a place like Alaska is an eye opener in terms of the possibilities for a place that's still got these large populations of animals. The window will always be open.

Source: "Bear of the Last Frontier: Interview with Chris Morgan." PBS. Thirteen, May 4, 2011. Web. Accessed May 10, 2016.

What's the Big Idea?

Take a close look at this text. What is the main point? Pick out two details used to make this point. What can you tell about grizzly bear populations based on this text?

CHAPTER TWO

TODAY'S GRIZZLY BEARS

Grizzly bears live in Alaska, Canada, and the northwestern 48 states. They can be found in a wide variety of habitats, including dense forests, open plains, and even the Arctic tundra.

Many grizzly bears are dark brown. They can be much lighter or darker, though. Some are even cream or black. Grizzly bear fur is often white at the tips. This feature gave the species its name. The bear's

The Denali tundra of Alaska is home to many grizzly bears.

Grizzlies get their name from their white-tipped hair.

fur is said to be grizzled, meaning it is streaked with gray. One of the ways to tell a grizzly from other bears is the grizzly's hump. This hump is actually a large shoulder muscle. The bear's hump and long claws help the animal dig for food.

Grizzlies are large animals. Most weigh between 200 and 700 pounds (90–320 kg). Very large males have rarely been known to reach 1,700 pounds (770 kg).

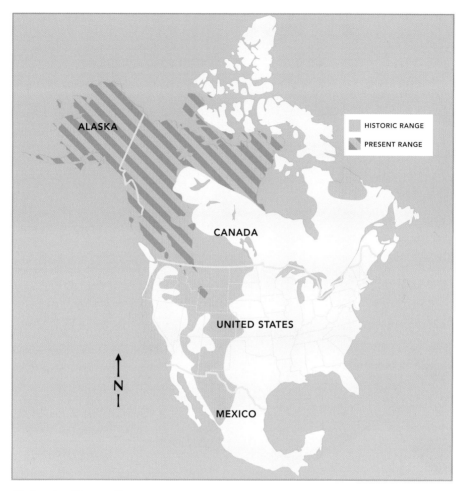

HISTORIC RANGE
PRESENT RANGE

ALASKA

CANADA

UNITED STATES

N

MEXICO

Grizzly Bear Range

This map shows the grizzly bear's current and historic ranges. What does this map tell you about how the species has changed over time?

Time to Rest

Most grizzly bears live less than 25 years. But some can live up to 30 years. When a bear is about five years old, it begins searching for a mate. Grizzlies

Grizzlies hibernate in dens. They may dig a den or use an existing cave.

mate in early summer. But the embryos do not develop right away. The mothers store up fat for the winter. If they gain enough weight, the embryos begin to develop in October or November. That is when grizzlies begin to hibernate. The embryos develop through January.

Grizzlies hibernate during the winter. This rest period saves an animal's energy when food is most scarce. The bears eat as much as they can during the summer and fall. Some gain as many as three pounds (1.4 kg) a day at this time. They then live off their stored fat reserves for up to seven months. They do not eat, drink, urinate, or defecate during hibernation.

Hibernation is not simply a deep sleep. Grizzly bears can wake up quickly if disturbed. Female grizzlies give birth to their young during hibernation, usually in January. The cubs nurse and sleep beside their mom. Staying inside

It Takes Time

Grizzly bears do not have cubs often. Most female grizzlies give birth only once every three years. They do not raise their young quickly. The cubs stay with their mother for two to three years. They rely on her for both food and protection as they grow. They also need her to teach them to find food on their own. Mother bears wait until one set of cubs is fully grown before having more cubs. This timetable makes it difficult for grizzly bears to bounce back easily from population losses.

the den gives the cubs a warm, safe place to start their lives.

Grizzlies leave their dens when the weather warms. Food is more available again. Adult males and females without cubs are often the first to leave their dens in the spring. Mothers with cubs are usually last.

A mother grizzly may give birth to one to four cubs. A pair of cubs is most common. These young bears stay with her until they are at least two years old. During this time she teaches them how to find food and take care of themselves.

Adults spend most of their lives alone. Some grizzlies rub their backs against trees to leave their scent behind. This lets other bears know they are nearby. But grizzly bears are not territorial. Adult bears may join together when there is plenty of food.

Finding Food

Grizzlies eat a variety of foods. They eat carcasses of animals, such as deer and elk. They will also eat berries, grasses, and seeds. Grizzly bears regularly eat insects, such as ants. A grizzly bear uses its nose to locate food. It can smell food from miles away.

Much of the bear's diet depends on where it lives. Grizzly bears can be found in forests, meadows, and the Alaskan tundra. Bears living near the ocean eat large amounts of salmon. Those living inland may eat trout. When food is hard to find, grizzlies can sometimes attack livestock. A bear may also follow its nose to nearby homes when it smells food in bird feeders or garbage cans. Grizzly bears are also drawn to fruit trees and bee yards. People keep hives in bee yards.

Athletes

Despite their size, grizzly bears are athletic. Adults can run at up to 35 miles per hour (55 km/h) over short distances. Grizzlies are also strong swimmers. Young cubs are skilled tree climbers when they need to escape danger. But this ability lessens with age. As their front claws grow longer, they get in the way of the bear's grip on the bark. Climbing becomes difficult, though not impossible. Adults' claws are excellent for finding food, though. They use their claws to dig for insects, pick fruits, and catch prey.

Many generations of grizzlies may use the same tree to leave their scent.

The hives produce honey. Bears that venture too close to farms and houses are often captured and relocated. They may be killed if they continue to seek foods around humans. Farmers depend on their animals for their livelihoods. Bears that wander nearby are considered a threat.

FURTHER EVIDENCE

Chapter Two contains information about the lives of grizzly bears. What do you think is the main point of the chapter? What evidence was given to support that point? Visit the website below to learn more about today's grizzly bears. Choose a quote from the website that relates to this chapter. Does this quote support the author's main point? Does it make a new point? Write a few sentences explaining how the quote you found relates to this chapter.

National Geographic: Grizzly Bear
mycorelibrary.com/grizzly-bears

CHAPTER THREE

THREATS

O ver the last two centuries, grizzly bears have faced a steady population decrease at the hands of humans. People moved into the animals' habitats. And when the bears tried to move across the humans' land in search of new habitats, many people killed them. By 1975 the grizzly population south of Canada dropped to just 2 percent of what it had been.

Bear-feeding stations at national parks during the early 1900s led to the killing of nuisance bears.

The Silver-Spoon Effect

Climate change has clear downsides. Warm weather has reduced the pine nut supply. But some grizzly bears are benefitting from warmer temperatures. When the weather is warmer, bears are able to build up more body fat before hibernation. This increases a mother's chances of giving birth to healthy cubs. Also, when the air remains warmer through the winter, these bears come out of their dens in the spring larger than bears that hibernated in regions with cooler winters. Scientists called this the silver-spoon effect. It has made it easier for some grizzlies to thrive.

Grizzly bear populations have increased since the animals were added to the Endangered Species List. The list categorized them as threatened. That meant they could soon be in danger of extinction. But grizzlies in the United States have lost approximately 98 percent of their original habitat. Many threats still exist.

Wandering into Town

Humans have built towns and roads where grizzly bears lived. This has led to conflicts between bears

All types of bears will wander into neighborhoods to find food.

and people. When bears roam into neighborhoods, they are considered dangerous. Attacks on people are rare, but the species is known for its aggressive behavior. When a grizzly feels threatened, it can

25

defend itself. This is especially true of female bears with cubs.

Many females unknowingly lead their cubs into danger. Grizzly bears will go wherever they must to find food. This behavior often leads them toward people. Once a bear discovers a good food source, such as a garbage can, it will revisit the area repeatedly. And the next time a mother bear comes, she often brings her hungry cubs. The mother bear is more likely to act aggressively if she feels her cubs are in danger.

Grizzlies versus Polar Bears

When bears are forced out of their habitats, they must go somewhere. Some displaced grizzlies have begun encroaching on other species. In northern Canada, they have recently moved into polar bear habitat. This move threatens polar bears and their cubs. Depending on the exact location, both grizzlies and polar bears are protected under law. And grizzly bears are unlikely to leave on their own. The region offers plenty of caribou, moose, fish, and berries.

In November 2015, people protested illegal hunting and poaching after hockey player Clayton Stoner was charged with killing a grizzly illegally.

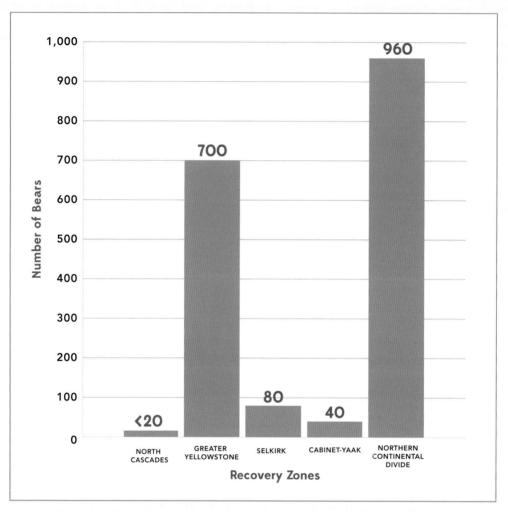

Rising Numbers

There are several grizzly bear recovery zones. These zones protect bears. This chart notes the location of each zone and its estimated population in the mid-2010s. Why do you think some zones have smaller populations than others?

Hunting

Humans are the cause of between 70 and 90 percent

of adult grizzly deaths in the US Rocky Mountains.

Some of these are killed illegally. Hunting is legal with a permit in Alaska and parts of Canada. The governments limit the number of bears that can be killed. Still, some people illegally hunt bears. Hunters may mistake a grizzly bear for a black bear and kill it without a license.

Poachers also kill grizzlies. Poachers are people who knowingly hunt animals illegally. They kill grizzlies for their fur, paws, and gallbladders. Some people believe that a bear's gallbladder has healing powers. Poachers will sell these organs overseas for as much as $3,000 each.

Dangerous Roads

Roads are another danger grizzly bears face. Some roads give people access to remote regions for logging and mining. These roads give poachers access to the bears. Roads have cut off many grizzly bear populations from one another. This has made it more difficult for the animals to reproduce. There are not always enough mates in one area.

Roads can be deadly for grizzly bears.

Cars can be deadly on roads. Bears that wander onto highways or other roads may be hit or killed. In 2015 three accidents involving grizzly bears occurred in northwest Montana in less than a week. In all three accidents, the bears died.

Many of the threats grizzlies face result from humans moving onto their land. Much of the bear's range is not protected. In Canada, laws protect only 7 percent of the species' range. But certain places, such as Yellowstone National Park and Grand Teton National Park, offer protected land for the bears.

EXPLORE ONLINE

The focus of Chapter Three was on threats that grizzly bears are still facing. The website below focuses on the same topic. As you know, every source is different. How is the information at the website different from the information in this chapter? What information is the same? What information did you learn from the website?

Official Griz Kills Threaten the Population
mycorelibrary.com/grizzly-bears

CHAPTER FOUR

THE FUTURE

The Endangered Species Act gave the grizzlies protection in 1975. At that time, only 136 grizzlies lived in the Greater Yellowstone Ecosystem. Conservationists knew if something didn't change soon, the species would go extinct. That year, the grizzly bear was listed as a threatened species. It was placed on the Endangered Species List. This helped save the species from extinction. This law

In 2014 there were as many as 839 grizzlies in Greater Yellowstone.

How to Prevent a Grizzly Attack

Knowing how to prevent an attack can save a bear's life. Campers should keep food far away from tents. They should hang food packs from a branch at least ten feet (3 m) off the ground. This branch should not be one other campers have used. Hikers should avoid carrying too much food. This might attract bears. Grizzly attacks are rare. Just 1 in 2.2 million people who visited Yellowstone National Park between 1980 and 2014 were attacked. But those who encounter a grizzly should stay perfectly quiet and still. They should not scream or run. They should carry bear spray made specifically to deter bears. This deterrent has been proven to prevent 90 percent of bear attacks.

protected bears from hunting and preserved their habitat. But it takes more than legal protection to keep grizzlies safe.

Conservation groups, such as Defenders of Wildlife, teach people how to keep bears off their property. Electric fencing can keep bears away from beehives, chicken coops, and other livestock. This keeps everyone safe.

People who live within the grizzly bear's range also have to be careful with garbage. Bear-resistant containers

Bear-proof garbage cans can keep bears out for more than 90 minutes.

can make a big difference. If the bears cannot smell or reach discarded food, it won't cause a problem. One of the best ways people can help bears is by avoiding interactions with them as much as possible.

Tracking Grizzlies

Scientists use Global Positioning System (GPS) radio collars to track certain grizzly bears. They capture a bear, fit it with a collar, and then release it. The collars track where the bears go. The collars also allow the researchers to find the same bears again. The researchers retrieve the collars and the data they have collected. One of the things they have learned is that bears cross roads often. They are most likely to cross when traffic is heavy. Researchers think this is because bears are most active during daylight hours. Collars have also shown that bears move along river systems. This information helps researchers learn how to help grizzly bears.

Grizzly Bears in the Lower 48 States

There are approximately 1,800 grizzly bears in the lower 48 states. Recovery zones in the Bitterroot Mountains of eastern Idaho and western Montana contained no grizzlies in 2016. Some biologists are hoping to fix this. They want to trap bears from areas where populations are higher. The scientists then plan to move the bears to these mountains where they can begin reproducing. Scientists think this region could

GPS collars give scientists information on population numbers and reproduction patterns.

Hunting in the Rocky Mountains

In March of 2016, the administration of President Barack Obama proposed delisting, or removing protections from, the grizzlies in the Yellowstone ecosystem. In this area the species has recovered enough to allow limited hunting. More than 700 bears currently live in and around Yellowstone. To make sure the change does not threaten the species, the states would agree to manage these hunts to just a few bears. This way numbers can be sustained. Hunting will end if the population drops below 600 bears. The US Fish and Wildlife Service planned to make the final decision on the matter in 2017. Even if the protections are dropped, however, the states may decide not to allow hunting.

support as many as 600 members of the species.

Bear managers have also worked to reunite bear populations without risking their lives. In the 1990s the Canadian government and Parks Canada began a project called the Banff Wildlife Crossings Project. It consisted of building 50 miles (80 km) of fencing in Canada to keep grizzly bears off a busy stretch of highway. The project also included 60 crossing structures so the bears could move from one side of the

The Banff wildlife overpasses give animals safe places to cross roads.

road to the other. Some of the crossings rise over the highways. Others tunnel under the roads. This enormous undertaking was completed in 2013. By 2014 the number of large mammals killed by traffic was down 80 percent.

The Future Looks Bright

Conservationists know the future for grizzly bears depends on their continuing work. Groups such as the National Wildlife Federation work to secure lands outside national parks. They make these lands better grizzly habitat. They use it to expand the bear's protected territory.

Scientists also continue to study grizzly populations. They will see if the species starts declining. Some conservation groups urge Congress to set aside money to help grizzly bear conservation. People are working hard to make sure the grizzly bear never becomes threatened again.

An article in *Yellowstone Science* describes studying grizzly bears in Yellowstone National Park. The work is never boring. It also isn't simple:

> One of the many benefits of studying grizzly bears in Yellowstone is they are a popular topic of conversation. . . . In such conversations about bears, 9 out of 10 times the first question is "How many grizzly bears are there?" . . . Although we usually have an answer, what's behind the answer is by no means simple. Like other elusive animals, grizzly bears are notoriously difficult to study. They occur in low densities, are active at times when observation is difficult (early morning and late evening), and use remote habitats and rough terrain. Only through a concerted, long-term research and monitoring effort have we begun to understand many fascinating aspects of grizzly bear population demographics (the statistical study of populations).

Source: Frank T. van Manen, Mark A. Haroldson, Dan D. Bjornlie, Cecily M. Costello, and Michael R. Ebinger. "Demographic Changes in Yellowstone's Grizzly Population." Yellowstone Science December 2015: 17–25. Print. 17.

Back It Up

The authors of this passage used evidence to support a point. Write a paragraph describing the point. Then write down two or three pieces of evidence the authors used to make the point.

SPECIES OVERVIEW

Common Name

- Grizzly bear

Scientific Name

- *Ursus arctos horribilis*

Average Size

- 5 to 8 feet (1.5–2.5 m) tall at the shoulder
- 200 to 700 pounds (90–320 kg)

Color

- Any shade of brown from cream to black, with white tips

Diet

- A wide variety of foods, including fish, berries, roots, insects, grasses, and seeds, as well as caribou, deer, moose, or elk carcasses

Average Life Span

- 15–30 years

Habitat

- Forests, grasslands, mountains, woodlands, and tundra

Threats

- Conflicts with humans, encroachment, hunting, and poaching
- Endangered status: Threatened

STOP AND THINK

Surprise Me

Chapter Two shared some interesting information about the grizzly bear species. After reading this book, what two or three facts from the chapter did you find most surprising? Why did you find each fact surprising?

Say What?

Learning about grizzly bears and conservation can mean learning a lot of new vocabulary. Find five words in this book you had never seen or heard before. Use a dictionary to find out what they mean. Then write the meanings in your own words and use each word in a new sentence.

Tell the Tale

Chapter Two discusses the lives of grizzly bears. Imagine you are a young grizzly bear. Write 200 words about what it is like to grow up as a grizzly bear. Make sure to set the scene, develop a sequence of events, and include a conclusion.

You Are There

This book discusses how grizzly bears hibernate. Imagine you are a grizzly bear preparing for winter. What might you eat? How might your body change between fall and spring? What do you think would be the hardest part of hibernation? Be sure to add plenty of detail to your notes.

GLOSSARY

conservation
preserving and protecting
something

ecologist
a person who studies the
relationships between living
things and the environment

embryo
the early developmental
stage of an animal before it is
born

encroach
to move onto another's
property

GPS
the Global Positioning
System, which uses satellites
to find the locations of
objects

hibernate
to spend the winter in a
restful state to save energy

poachers
people who illegally hunt wild
animals

range
an area where an animal lives

species
a group of animals or plants
that share basic traits

subspecies
a group of animals within a
species that share basic traits
different from the rest of the
species

territory
an area where animals live
and find food

tundra
a treeless plain in the arctic

LEARN MORE

Books

Hoare, Ben, and Tom Jackson. *Endangered Animals.* New York: DK Publishing, 2010.

McCarthy, Cecilia Pinto. *Yellowstone National Park.* Minneapolis, MN: Abdo Publishing, 2017.

Sartore, Joel. *Face to Face with Grizzlies.* Washington, DC: National Geographic, 2007.

Websites

To learn more about Back from Near Extinction, visit **booklinks.abdopublishing.com**. These links are routinely monitored and updated to provide the most current information available.

Visit **mycorelibrary.com** for free additional tools for teachers and students.

INDEX

ABOUT THE AUTHOR

Tammy Gagne has written more than 150 books for adults and children. She resides in northern New England with her husband and son. One of her favorite pastimes is visiting schools to talk to kids about the writing process.